KIDS' SPORTS STORIES

HORSE SHOW SWITCH

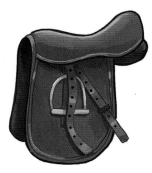

by Cari Meister

illustrated by Alex Patrick

PICTURE WINDOW BOOKS
a capstone imprint

Published by Picture Window Books,
an imprint of Capstone.
1710 Roe Crest Drive
North Mankato, Minnesota 56003
capstonepub.com

Library of Congress Cataloging-in-Publication Data is available
on the Library of Congress website.
ISBN: 9781663909503 (hardcover)
ISBN: 9781663921284 (paperback)
ISBN: 9781663909473 (ebook PDF)

Summary: Imani loves riding her lesson pony, Peanut. They make a great team. But before
the big show, Peanut starts limping and needs to rest. Imani's instructor offers to let her
ride a different horse, Rico, for the upcoming show. But Rico is much bigger and faster
than Peanut, and Imani is nervous. Will she be able to compete on show day?

Designer: Tracy Davies

Printed and bound in the USA. 4270

TABLE OF CONTENTS

GLOSSARY

 **arena**—an oval-shaped ring where people ride horses

 **class**—an event in which riders compete

 **lame**—having an injury

 **reins**—the part of the bridle that you hold when riding a horse; reins help steer a horse

 **saddle**—a seat for a rider on the back of a horse

Chapter 1
PEANUT NEEDS TO REST

"I can't wait for our lesson today!" said Imani.

She leaned toward her pony's neck. "You've been listening so well, haven't you, Peanut? We are going to do great in the show coming up!"

Group lesson days were Imani's favorite. She loved riding with her friends, Peter and Reese.

After they got ready, the three friends rode their horses into the **arena**.

Their trainer, Jess, sat on a stool in the middle.

"Let's warm up," said Jess. "Walk around the arena three times. Keep your **reins** long so your horses can stretch their necks."

After they were done, Jess said, "Now trot your horses."

Imani squeezed her legs to get Peanut to trot. But something felt wrong. The horse tripped. Then he went back to a walk.

Imani squeezed again. Peanut trotted.

But he was limping!

"Jess," called Imani. "Something's wrong with Peanut."

Jess watched. "He's **lame**," she said. "Go see if Dr. Zee is here."

Imani took Peanut back to the barn and found the vet. The vet looked closely at Peanut. "He has a sprain," said Dr. Zee. "He'll be fine. But he needs a month of rest."

Imani frowned. The horse show was
in two weeks. Now she couldn't compete.
She fought back tears as she patted
Peanut's neck.

Chapter 2

A NEW HORSE

The next day, Imani went to check on Peanut. She was feeding him carrots when Jess walked into the barn.

"Hi, Imani," said Jess. "Do you want to ride Rico at the show?"

Imani's eyes widened. Rico! Rico was Jess's horse. He was *much* bigger than Peanut.

"Why don't you try him in the lesson today?" said Jess.

"Good idea!" called Reese from one stall
over. "You should ride Rico!"

Imani wasn't so sure.

"I'll hold him while you get up," said Jess.

"He's so big!" said Imani. "But I'll try."

Imani grabbed the front of the **saddle** and got up—way up!

"Wow! I'm really high!" Imani said. She smiled, but she felt a little afraid.

"I'll lead him until you get used to the
way he moves," said Jess.

Imani nodded slowly.

"You look good on him!" said Peter.

"Thanks!" said Imani.

Jess walked Rico around. Rico felt very different from Peanut. His strides were long and smooth. But soon Imani got used to him, and she began riding on her own.

Maybe I can do the horse show after all, she thought.

After almost two weeks of riding Rico,
Imani was no longer nervous.

"We'll do great tomorrow," she told him
the night before the show.

Rico neighed.

Chapter 3
SHOW TIME

Imani's mom picked up Reese early the next morning. The girls chatted in the car.

"Did you bring treats for the horses?" asked Reese.

"I sure did!" said Imani, pointing to her bag.

When they got there, Jess and Peter were already there with the horses.

But when Imani saw Rico, she froze.

Rico was stamping and tossing his head.

"What's wrong?" Imani asked softly.

"He's a little nervous," said Jess. "He hasn't been to a show recently. He'll be fine."

Imani wasn't so sure. She had never seen Rico like this.

"Brush him," said Jess. "Then walk him. He'll calm down."

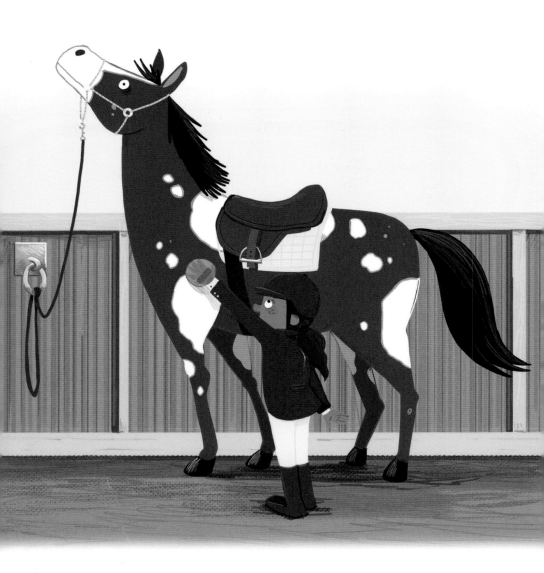

Imani brushed Rico. Then she walked
him. He calmed a bit, but he wouldn't stop
flipping his head. Imani got more and
more uneasy. Her stomach started to hurt.

Soon it was time for the first **class**.

"I don't know if I can ride Rico like this," Imani said to Jess.

"If he gets to be too hard to handle," said Jess, "just get off and walk him out."

Imani walked into the ring. She lined up
behind Reese and Peter.

Rico would not stand still. "Easy," Imani
whispered.

The announcer called out, "Riders, walk your horses to the left."

Imani sat up tall. She squeezed her legs to get Rico to walk. But Rico didn't walk. He started trotting—fast!

Imani pulled back on the reins. "Easy, Rico," she whispered. "Just walk."

She steered Rico to the rail, and he did better. But when the announcer called for a trot, Rico spooked. He sidestepped. Imani bounced out of the saddle. She felt out of control. She thought of quitting.

Then she took a deep breath. She used the inside of her leg to push Rico back to the rail. *I can do this*, Imani thought.

When the class was over, she walked out
of the ring.

"Way to stick with him!" said Jess.

Imani smiled.

Poles were next. Rico tripped over the first two poles, but he trotted over the other ones perfectly.

Soon the class was over. Peter, Reese, and Imani all went home with ribbons!

"I knew we could do it!" said Imani.

O SE SHOW FU

Pretend that you are going to a horse show with this fun activity. You can play it alone or with friends.

What You Need:
- rope, string, branches, or other long, straight objects
- yard stick or broom
- award prizes

What You Do:
- If you have long hair, pull it back neatly. In many horse-riding competitions, riders pull their hair back to keep it out of the way. This also helps give them a polished look.
- Set up a poles course. You can use rope, string, branches, or anything else you can find to be the "poles."
- Grab a yard stick or a broom. This will be your "horse." You can even name your horse if you like.
- Now ride the poles course. First step over all of the poles. Then try jumping over them. If you play with friends, you can give each other scores. Award winners with prizes or blue ribbons!

REPLAY IT!

Take another look at this illustration. How do you think Imani felt when Rico wasn't listening? How would you feel?

Now pretend you are Imani. Write a letter to your friend about your first class with Rico. Make sure to write about how you felt after finishing the class.

ABOUT THE AUTHOR

Cari Meister is the author of more than 100 books for children, including the Fairy Hill series and the Tiny series. She lives with her family in Vail, Colorado. Cari enjoys yoga, horseback riding, and skiing. You can visit her online at carimeister.com.

ABOUT THE ILLUSTRATOR

Alex Patrick was born in the Kentish town of Dartford in the southeast of England. He has been drawing for as long as he can remember. His lifelong love for cartoons, picture books, and comics has shaped him into the passionate children's illustrator he is today. Alex loves creating original characters. He brings an element of fun and humor to each of his illustrations and is often found laughing to himself as he draws.